Little Frog and the
dog
THE BOOK PROJECT
by Martin Waddell
Illustrated by Trevor Dunton
BOW
WOW
WOW
WOW

This book is part of

THE LONGMAN BOOK PROJECT

General Editor: Sue Palmer
Fiction Editor: Wendy Body
Non-fiction Editor: Bobbie Neate

LONGMAN GROUP UK LIMITED
Longman House, Burnt Mill, Harlow, Essex, CM20 2JE, England and
Associated Companies throughout the World.

First published 1994
ISBN 0 582 12139 6
Second impression 1995

Set in Lefrut 18/26pt (Linotronic)

Produced by Longman Singapore Publishers Pte Ltd
Printed in Singapore

The publisher's policy is to use paper manufactured from sustainable forests.

Little Frog and the dog

by Martin Waddell

Illustrated by Trevor Dunton

Little Frog was out frogging one day when ...

Little Frog met a dog!
Bow-wow-wow-wow!!

Hop-hop-plop!
Little Frog got away.

Little Frog thought he could be a Frog-dog.

So he found a Frog-horn and went Bow-wow-wow-wow!

Auntie Frog was asleep on a log.

Bow-wow-wow-wow!
Little Frog frightened
Auntie and Auntie Frog
jumped off the log!

Old Bull Frog was up on the bank.

Bow-wow-wow-wow!
Little Frog frightened Old
Bull Frog and Old Bull Frog
jumped in the mud!

Sister Frog sat on a lily.

Bow-wow-wow-wow!

Little Frog frightened Sister Frog

and Sister Frog jumped in the lake!

Little Frog laughed and laughed.

But Bull Frog and Auntie and Sister didn't think it was funny!
They crept up behind Little Frog.

Bow-wow-wow-wow!
Hop-hop-hop-hop-blatt!

"That just serves you right, Little Frog!" Auntie Frog said.

Some other books by Martin Waddell

The Great Green Mouse Disaster
published by Anderson and Beaver

Can't You Sleep Little Bear?
published by Walker Books Limited

Once There Were Giants
published by Walker Books Limited

The Hidden House
published by Walker Books Limited

Grandma's Bill
published by Simon & Schuster

Farmer Duck
published by Walker Books Limited

Little Frog and the dog

Read-Aloud Book

A frog in the throat

Read-On Books

Little Frog and the dog

Little Frog and the tadpoles

Little Frog and the Frog Olympics